Peppa Pig™

CREATE BY STICKER
STORYBOOK
FAVORITE CHARACTERS

Adapted by Cala Spinner

SCHOLASTIC INC.

ISBN 978-1-338-61173-1

10 9 8 7 6 5 4 3 2 1   20 21 22 23 24
Printed in Malaysia   106

First edition 2020

By Cala Spinner
Book design by Jessica Meltzer
Additional illustrations by Jason Fruchter

MESSY FUN!

Peppa's world can be a little . . . messy!
In this book, you will read a story about Peppa
Pig. Then match the stickers in the back of
the book to their missing spots on the pages.

Turn the pages to complete the next one,
and the next one, and the next!

Puzzle Page

Use the stickers on page 31 to complete the
image of Peppa as a fairy!

Sticker Page

Fairy Peppa

Tomorrow is a special day at school. The children will **dress up** as their favorite book characters!

"Can I come as someone from a **fairy tale**?" asks Candy Cat.

"Yes," Madame Gazelle says. "You can dress up as a character from any book you'd like."

Use the stickers on page 25 to complete the image of **Candy Cat** as a fairy-tale character!

1

4

2

6

5 7 3

Peppa is excited. She can't wait to dress up tomorrow!
"Who are you going to be, Peppa?" asks Mummy Pig.
"You've got lots of books to choose from," says
Daddy Pig.
Peppa does have lots of choices! She can go as a
princess.

Use the stickers on page 27 to complete the image of Peppa as a princess!

Or she can go as a **duck!**

Use the stickers on page 29 to complete an image
of the duck!

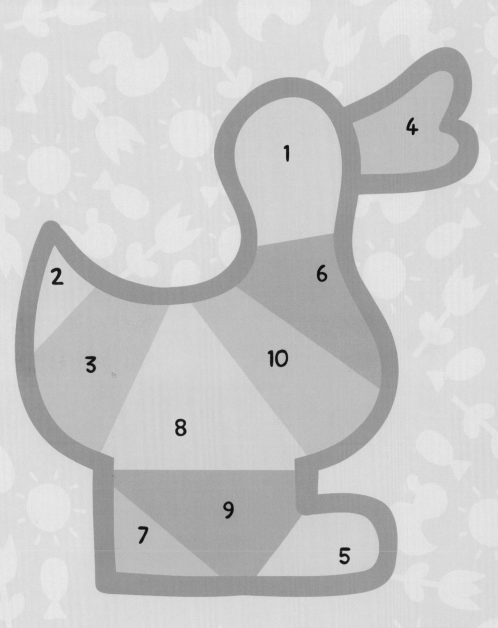

"Hmm," says Mummy Pig. "How about this book?"
She holds up *The Tiny Magic Fairy*.
"Hee! Hee! Hee!" Peppa laughs.
It's perfect! She can't wait.

Use the stickers on page 31 to complete the
image of Peppa as a fairy!

Now it is George's turn.
"What's your favorite book?" asks Mummy Pig.
"Dine-saw! Grr!" says George.
"Of course!" says Daddy Pig.
"Your pop-up book!"

Use the stickers on page 33 to complete the image of George's favorite green dinosaur!

"That's settled then," says Mummy Pig. "George will go as a dinosaur and Peppa will go as a fairy."

But while brushing her teeth, Peppa isn't so sure. Maybe she wants to be a pirate?

"Oh no," Peppa says. "My favorite book keeps changing!"

Use the stickers on page 35 to complete the image of Peppa as a pirate!

The next day at school, the children arrive all dressed up.

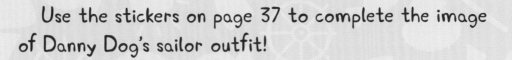

Use the stickers on page 37 to complete the image of Danny Dog's sailor outfit!

Everyone has exciting and marvelous costumes.
But what is Peppa?

Use the stickers on page 39 to complete the image of Peppa's outfit!

"I am all my favorite books!" Peppa says. "I have fairy wings, tee-hee! A pirate hat, ARR! And quack quack, duck feet!"

"Hee hee!" laughs Suzy Sheep. "You're a fairy-pirate-duck!"

Use the stickers on page 41 to complete the image
of Suzy Sheep's outfit!

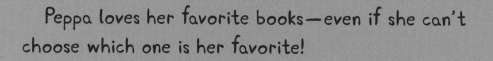

Peppa loves her favorite books—even if she can't choose which one is her favorite!

Use the stickers on page 43 to complete Pedro Pony's outfit!

Candy Cat

Princess Peppa

Duck

Use the stickers on page 29 to complete an image of the duck!

Fairy Peppa

Use the stickers on page 31 to complete the image of Peppa as a fairy!

31

Use the stickers on page 33 to complete the image of George's favorite green dinosaur!

13

George's Dinosaur

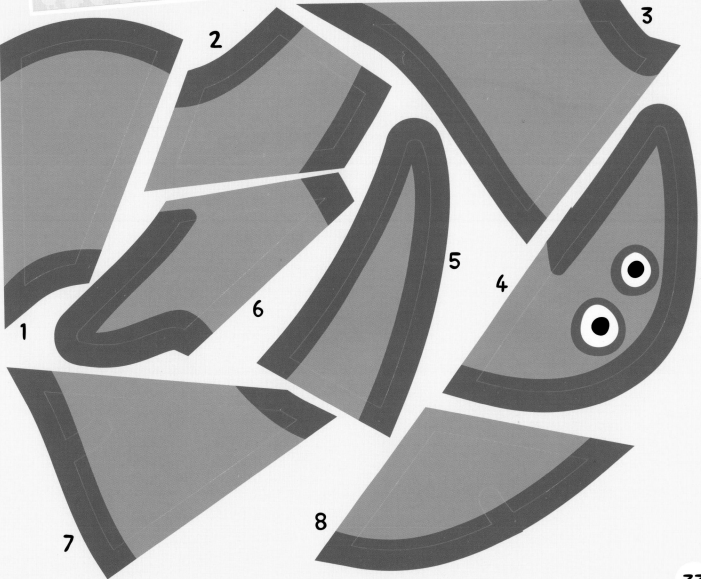

Pirate Peppa

Danny Dog

Use the stickers on page 37 to complete the image of Danny Dog's sailor outfit!

Peppa Pig

Use the stickers on page 39 to complete the image of Peppa's outfit!

Suzy Sheep